Bonnie Larkin Nims

Where Is the Bear at School?

Pictures by **Madelaine Gill**

ALBERT WHITMAN & COMPANY, NILES, ILLINOIS

ALSO BY BONNIE NIMS
Where Is the Bear?

Text © 1989 by Bonnie Larkin Nims
Illustrations © 1989 by Madelaine Gill
Published in 1989 by Albert Whitman & Company,
5747 West Howard Street,
Niles, Illinois 60648.
Published simultaneously in Canada by
General Publishing, Limited, Toronto.
All rights reserved.
Printed in the United States of America.
10 9 8 7 6 5 4 3 2 1

Library of Congress Cataloging-in Publication Data
Nims, Bonnie Larkin.
Where is the bear at school? / Bonnie Larkin Nims;
illustrated by Madelaine Gill.
p. cm.
Summary: Rhyming text asks the reader to find, with increasing
degrees of difficulty, the hidden bear in each scene.
ISBN 0-8075-8935-7 (lib. bdg.)
[1. Bears—Fiction.   2. Literary recreations.   3. Picture puzzles.
4. Stories in rhyme.]   I. Gill, Madelaine, ill.   II. Title.
PZ8.3.N6Wi 1989   89-37903
[E]—dc20   CIP
                                                               AC

For James, Jeremy, Elliot, & Company. *B.N.*

To Rosemary, Kate, & Gillian,
with thanks for all their great help! *M.G.*

School is a place
where a bear
can *really* hide!
If you don't believe it,
try to find him inside. . .

I see caps, coats, and mittens,
and pegs to hang them on,
and a sleepyhead rubbing her eyes
while trying to swallow a yawn.

But I am looking for a bear.
Can you show me—
where is the bear?

There's the teacher reading a story
about a little red hen,
and the children so happy to hear it,
they'll want to hear it again.

But I am looking for a bear.
Can you show me—
where is the bear?

I see lots of smocks with lots of spots—
red, yellow, blue—
Which are painters? Which are paints?
I can't tell, can you?

But I am looking for a bear.
Can you show me—
where is the bear?

I see children teeter-tottering,
sliding on the slide, swinging on the swing,
running, jumping, hiding, seeking,
and dancing around in a ring.

But I am looking for a bear.
Can you show me—
where is the bear?

I see lunch with cookies and fruit,
someone who's hungry, someone who's not,
and someone making an awful face
who doesn't like what he's got!

But I am looking for a bear.
Can you show me—
where is the bear?

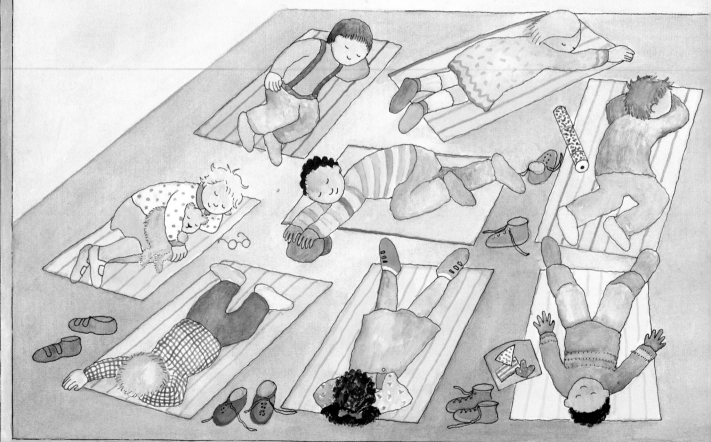

I see children taking a nap,
lying on mats in different poses—
all scrunched up or flat out wide,
or hiding their stomachs and noses.

But I am looking for a bear.
Can you show me—
where is the bear?

I see drums tum-a-ta-tumming,
tamborines ching-a-cha-chinging,
whistles whee-oh-whee wheeing,
triangles ting-a-ling-linging.

But I am looking for a bear.
Can you show me—
where is the bear?

There's a cowgirl, a pirate,
a ghost, and a queen,
a friendly lion, another ghost,
and the BIGGEST BEE EVER SEEN!

But I am looking for a bear.
Can you show me—
where is the bear?

I see lots of people, big and small,
waving goodbye, waving hello.
"School's over," they're saying,
"it's time for us to go!"

But I am looking for a bear.
Can you show me—
where is the bear?

Bonnie Nims is the author of three books for young people and numerous stories and poems. She was editor-in-chief of an eighteen-volume children's encyclopedia, and her work has appeared widely in reading and humanities textbooks.

While reading Bonnie's book *Where Is the Bear?* her two-and-a-half-year-old friend Elise P. explained, "I like this book because I get to use my fingers!" This is precisely the author's intention—to write books that are active experiences attracting even the youngest readers.

Bonnie and her husband, the poet John Frederick Nims, live in Chicago in a tall apartment building where they enjoy a view of two natural wonders—Lake Michigan and a children's playground.

Madelaine Gill has written and illustrated *Under the Blanket* and illustrated several other books for children. She lives in New York City with her daughter, Gillian, and a cat named Kitty, King of the Coconuts—or Coconut, for short.

While working on the illustrations for *Where Is the Bear at School?* Madelaine, Gillian, and Coconut stayed at Gillian's grandparents' house in the country, and Coconut learned how to live in the same home with three dogs and three birds. Like the bear in this book, he became an expert at hiding.